Defoe Abbott Marx Hardy Machiavelli Montaigne Chesterton Cooper Emerson Joyce Austen Hugo Eliot Grimm Melville Carroll Christie Haggard Molière Stoker Wilde Maupassant Byron Schiller Garnett Einstein Fitzgerald Engels Hall Kafka Goethe Hawthorne Smith Cotton Dostoyevsky Willis Baum Henry Kipling Doyle Leslie Dumas Flaubert Nietzsche Turgenev Balzac Stockton Vatsyayana Crane Burroughs Verne Curtis Tocqueville Gogol Vinci Homer Widger Tolstoy Whitman Busch Darwin Thoreau Twain Scott Potter Freud Zola Plato Harte Kant Jowett Stevenson Lawrence Dickens Hesse Andersen Cervantes Burton London Descartes Voltaire Poe Aristotle Wells Hale James Hastings Cooke Bunner Shakespeare Irving Richter Chekhov Chambers da Shaw Wodehouse Doré Dante Swift Benedict Alcott Pushkin Newton

Rose and Roof-Tree

Poems

George Parsons Lathrop

Imprint

This book is part of TREDITION CLASSICS

Author: George Parsons Lathrop
Cover design: Buchgut, Berlin – Germany

Publisher: tredition GmbH, Hamburg - Germany
ISBN: 978-3-8424-2915-4

www.tredition.com
www.tredition.de

ROSE AND ROOF-TREE:

POEMS

by

GEORGE PARSONS LATHROP

Upon the enchanted ladder of his rhymes,
    Round after round and patiently
    The poet ever upward climbs.

DEDICATION.

I need give my verse no hint as to whom it sings for. The rose, knowing her own right, makes servitors of the light-rays to carry her color. So every line here shall in some sense breathe of thee, and in its very face bear record of her whom, however unworthily, it seeks to serve and honor.

WINDFALLS.

ROSE AND ROOF-TREE.

O wayward rose, why dost thou wreathe so high,
Wasting thyself in sweet-breath'd ecstasy?

"The pulses of the wind my life uplift,
And through my sprays I feel the sunlight sift;

"And all my fibres, in a quick consent
Entwined, aspire to fill their heavenward bent.

"I feel the shaking of the far-off sea,
And all things growing blend their life with me:

"When men and women on me look, there glows
Within my veins a life not of the rose.

"Then let me grow, until I touch the sky,
And let me grow and grow until I die!"

So, every year, the sweet rose shooteth higher,
And scales the roof upon its wings of fire,

And pricks the air, in lovely discontent,
With thorns that question still of its intent.

But when it reached the roof-tree, there it clung,
Nor ever farther up its blossoms flung.

O wayward rose, why hast thou ceased to climb?
Hast thou forgot the ardor of thy prime?

"O hearken!" — thus the rose-spray, listening, —
"With what weird music sweet these full hearts ring!

"What mazy ripples of deep, eddying sound,
 Rise, touch the roof-tree old, and drift around,

"Bearing aloft the burden musical
 Of joys and griefs from human hearts that fall!

"Green stem and fair, flush'd circle I will lay
 Along the roof, and listen here alway;

"For rose and tree, and every leafy growth
 That toward the sky unfolds with spiry blowth,

"No purpose hath save this, to breathe a grace
 O'er men, and in men's hearts to seek a place.

"Therefore, O poet, thou who gav'st to me
 The homage of thy humble sympathy,

"No longer vest thy verse in rose-leaves frail: —
 Let the heart's voice loud through thy pæan wail!"

   * * * * *

Lo, at my feet the wind of autumn throws
A hundred turbulent blossoms of the rose,

Full of the voices of the sea and grove
And air, and full of hidden, murmured love,

And warm with passion through the roof-tree sent;
Dew-drenched with tears;—all in one wild gush spent!

MUSIC OF GROWTH.

Music is in all growing things;
And underneath the silky wings
  Of smallest insects there is stirred
  A pulse of air that must be heard.
Earth's silence lives, and throbs, and sings.

If poet from the vibrant strings
Of his poor heart a measure flings,
  Laugh not, that he no trumpet blows:
  It may be that Heaven hears and knows
His language of low listenings.

A SONG LONG AGO.

Through the pauses of thy fervid singing
      Fell crystal sound
That thy fingers from the keys were flinging
      Lightly around:
I felt the vine-like harmonies close clinging
      About my soul;
And to my eyes, as fruit of their sweet bringing,
      The full tear stole!

MELANCHOLY.

Daughter of my nobler hope
  That dying gave thee birth,
    Sweet Melancholy!
  For memory of the dead,
  In her dear stead,
    'Bide thou with me,
    Sweet Melancholy!
As purple shadows to the tree,
When the last sun-rays sadly slope
Athwart the bare and darkening earth,
    Art thou to me,
    Sweet Melancholy!

CONTENTMENT.

  Glad hours have been when I have seen
    Life's scope and each dry day's intent
  United; so that I could stand
  In silence, covering with my hand
  The circle of the universe,
  Balance the blessing and the curse,
  And trust in deeds without chagrin,
Free from to-morrow and yesterday — content.

PART FIRST.

AN APRIL ARIA.

When the mornings dankly fall
  With a dim forethought of rain,
And the robins richly call
To their mates mercurial,
  And the tree-boughs creak and strain
    In the wind;
When the river's rough with foam,
  And the new-made clearings smoke,
And the clouds that go and come
Shine and darken frolicsome,
  And the frogs at evening croak
    Undefined
Mysteries of monotone,
  And by melting beds of snow
Wind-flowers blossom all alone;
    Then I know
That the bitter winter's dead.
    Over his head
The damp sod breaks so mellow,—
Its mosses tipped with points of yellow,—
  I cannot but be glad;
Yet this sweet mood will borrow
Something of a sweeter sorrow,
  To touch and turn me sad.

THE BOBOLINK.

How sweetly sang the bobolink,
  When thou, my Love, wast nigh!
His liquid music from the brink
Of some cloud-fountain seemed to sink,
  Built in the blue-domed sky.

How sadly sings the bobolink!
  No more my Love is nigh:
Yet rise, my spirit, rise, and drink
Once more from that cloud-fountain's brink, —
  Once more before I die!

THE SUN-SHOWER.

A penciled shade the sky doth sweep,
And transient glooms creep in to sleep
    Amid the orchard;
Fantastic breezes pull the trees
Hither and yon, to vagaries

    Of aspect tortured.
Then, like the downcast dreamy fringe
Of eyelids, when dim gates unhinge
    That locked their tears,
Falls on the hills a mist of rain, —
So faint, it seems to fade again;
    Yet swiftly nears.

Now sparkles the air, all steely-bright,
With drops swept down in arrow-flight,
    Keen, quivering lines.
Ceased in a breath the showery sound;
And teasingly, now, as I look around,
    Sweet sunlight shines!

JUNE LONGINGS.

Lo, all about the lofty blue are blown
Light vapors white, like thistle-down,
That from their softened silver heaps opaque
Scatter delicate flake by flake,
Upon the wide loom of the heavens weaving
Forms of fancies past believing,
And, with fantastic show of mute despair,
As for some sweet hope hurt beyond repair,
Melt in the silent voids of sunny air.

All day the cooing brooklet runs in tune:
Half sunk i' th' blue, the powdery moon
Shows whitely. Hark, the bobolink's note! I hear it,
Far and faint as a fairy spirit!
Yet all these pass, and as some blithe bird, winging,
Leaves a heart-ache for his singing,
A frustrate passion haunts me evermore
For that which closest dwells to beauty's core.
O Love, canst thou this heart of hope restore?

A RUNE OF THE RAIN.

I.

O many-toned rain!
O myriad sweet voices of the rain!
How welcome is its delicate overture
At evening, when the glowing-moistur'd west
Seals all things with cool promise of night's rest!

At first it would allure
The earth to kinder mood,
With dainty flattering

Of soft, sweet pattering:
Faintly now you hear the tramp
Of the fine drops falling damp
On the dry, sun-seasoned ground
And the thirsty leaves around.
But anon, imbued
With a sudden, bounding access
Of passion, it relaxes
All timider persuasion,
And, with nor pretext nor occasion,
Its wooing redoubles;
And pounds the ground, and bubbles
In sputtering spray,
Flinging itself in a fury
Of flashing white away;
Till the dusty road
Flings a perfume dank abroad,
And the grass, and the wide-hung trees,
The vines, the flowers in their beds,
The vivid corn that to the breeze
Rustles along the garden-rows,
Visibly lift their heads,—
And, as the shower wilder grows,
Upleap with answering kisses to the rain.

Then, the slow and pleasant murmur
Of its subsiding,
As the pulse of the storm beats firmer,
And the steady rain
Drops into a cadenced chiding.
Deep-breathing rain,
The sad and ghostly noise
Wherewith thou dost complain,—
Thy plaintive, spiritual voice,
Heard thus at close of day
Through vaults of twilight-gray,—
Doth vex me with sweet pain!
And still my soul is fain

To know the secret of that yearning
Which in thine utterance I hear returning.

Hush, oh hush!
Break not the dreamy rush
Of the rain:
Touch not the marring doubt
Words bring, to the certainty
Of its soft refrain,
But let the flying fringes flout
Their gouts against the pane,
And the gurgling throat of the water-spout
Groan in the eaves amain.

The earth is wedded to the shower.
Darkness and awe, gird round the bridal-hour!

II.

O many-tonèd rain!
It hath caught the strain
Of a wilder tune,
Ere the same night's noon,
When dreams and sleep forsake me,
And sudden dread doth wake me,
To hear the booming drums of heaven beat
The long roll to battle; when the knotted cloud,
With an echoing loud,
Bursts asunder
At the sudden resurrection of the thunder;
And the fountains of the air,
Unsealed again sweep, ruining, everywhere,
To wrap the world in a watery winding-sheet.

III.

O myriad sweet voices of the rain!
When the airy war doth wane,
And the storm to the east hath flown,
Cloaked close in the whirling wind,
There's a voice still left behind
In each heavy-hearted tree,
Charged with tearful memory
Of the vanished rain:
From their leafy lashes wet
Drip the dews of fresh regret
For the lover that's gone!
All else is still.
But the stars are listening;
And low o'er the wooded hill
Hangs, upon listless wing
Outspread, a shape of damp, blue cloud,
Watching, like a bird of evil
That knows no mercy nor reprieval,
The slow and silent death of the pallid moon.

IV.

But soon, returning duly,
Dawn whitens the wet hill-tops bluely.
To her vision pure and cold
The night's wild tale is told
On the glistening leaf, in the mid-road pool,
The garden mold turned dark and cool,
And the meadow's trampled acres.
But hark, how fresh the song of the winged music-makers!
For now the moanings bitter,
Left by the rain, make harmony
With the swallow's matin-twitter,
And the robin's note, like the wind's in a tree:
The infant morning breathes sweet breath,
And with it is blent

The wistful, wild, moist scent
Of the grass in the marsh which the sea nourisheth:
And behold!
The last reluctant drop of the storm,
Wrung from the roof, is smitten warm
And turned to gold;
For in its veins doth run
The very blood of the bold, unsullied sun!

THE SONG-SPARROW.

Glimmers gray the leafless thicket
  Close beside my garden gate,
Where, so light, from post to picket
  Hops the sparrow, blithe, sedate;
    Who, with meekly folded wing,
    Comes to sun himself and sing.

It was there, perhaps, last year,
  That his little house he built;
For he seems to perk and peer,
  And to twitter, too, and tilt
    The bare branches in between,
    With a fond, familiar mien.

Once, I know, there was a nest,
  Held there by the sideward thrust
Of those twigs that touch his breast;
  Though 'tis gone now. Some rude gust
    Caught it, over-full of snow, —
    Bent the bush, — and robbed it so

Thus our highest holds are lost,
  By the ruthless winter's wind,

When, with swift-dismantling frost,
  The green woods we dwelt in, thinn'd
    Of their leafage, grow too cold
    For frail hopes of summer's mold.

But if we, with spring-days mellow,
  Wake to woeful wrecks of change,
And the sparrow's ritornello
  Scaling still its old sweet range;
    Can we do a better thing
    Than, with him, still build and sing?

Oh, my sparrow, thou dost breed
  Thought in me beyond all telling;
Shootest through me sunlight, seed,
  And fruitful blessing, with that welling
    Ripple of ecstatic rest,
    Gurgling ever from thy breast!

And thy breezy carol spurs
  Vital motion in my blood,
Such as in the sapwood stirs,
  Swells and shapes the pointed bud
    Of the lilac; and besets
    The hollows thick with violets.

Yet I know not any charm
  That can make the fleeting time
Of thy sylvan, faint alarm
  Suit itself to human rhyme:
    And my yearning rhythmic word,
    Does thee grievous wrong, dear bird.

So, however thou hast wrought
  This wild joy on heart and brain,
It is better left untaught.

Take thou up the song again:
  There is nothing sad afloat
  On the tide that swells thy throat!

FAIRHAVEN BAY.

I push on through the shaggy wood,
I round the hill: 't is here it stood;
And there, beyond the crumbled walls,
The shining Concord slowly crawls,

Yet seems to make a passing stay,
And gently spreads its lilied bay,
Curbed by this green and reedy shore,
Up toward the ancient homestead's door.

But dumbly sits the shattered house,
And makes no answer: man and mouse
Long since forsook it, and decay
Chokes its deep heart with ashes gray.

On what was once a garden-ground
Dull red-bloomed sorrels now abound;
And boldly whistles the shy quail
Within the vacant pasture's pale.

Ah, strange and savage, where he shines,
The sun seems staring through those pines
That once the vanished home could bless
With intimate, sweet loneliness.

The ignorant, elastic sod
The feet of them that daily trod
Its roods hath utterly forgot:

The very fire-place knows them not.

For, in the weedy cellar, thick
The ruined chimney's mass of brick
Lies strown. Wide heaven, with such an ease
Dost thou, too, lose the thought of these?

Yet I, although I know not who
Lived here, in years that voiceless grew
Ere I was born, — and never can, —
Am moved, because I am a man.

Oh glorious gift of brotherhood!
Oh sweet elixir in the blood,
That makes us live with those long dead,
Or hope for those that shall be bred

Hereafter! No regret can rob
My heart of this delicious throb;
No thought of fortunes haply wrecked,
Nor pang for nature's wild neglect.

And, though the hearth be cracked and cold,
Though ruin all the place enfold,
These ashes that have lost their name
Shall warm my life with lasting flame!

CHANT FOR AUTUMN.

Veiled in visionary haze,
Behold, the ethereal autumn days
  Draw near again!
  In broad array,
With a low, laborious hum
These ministers of plenty come,

That seem to linger, while they steal away.

    O strange, sweet charm
    Of peaceful pain,
When yonder mountain's bended arm
Seems wafting o'er the harvest-plain
A message to the heart that grieves,
And round us, here, a sad-hued rain
Of leaves that loosen without number
Showering falls in yellow, umber,
Red, or russet, 'thwart the stream!
Now pale Sorrow shall encumber
All too soon these lands, I deem;
    Yet who at heart believes
    The autumn, a false friend,
    Can bring us fatal harm?
Ah, mist-hung avenues in dream
Not more uncertainly extend
    Than the season that receives
    A summer's latest gleam!

But the days of death advance:
  They tarry not, nor turn!
I will gather the ashes of summer
  In my heart, as an urn.

    Oh draw thou nearer,
     Thou
Spirit of the distant height,
Whither now that slender flight
Of swallows, winging, guides my sight!
    The hill cloth seem to me
    A fading memory
      Of long delight,
    And in its distant blue
    Half hideth from my view
This shrinking season that must now retire;

And so shall hold it, hopeful, a desire
And knowledge old as night and always new.
  Draw nigher! And, with bended brow,
    I will be thy reverer
    Through the long winter's term!

So, when the snows hold firm,
    And the brook is dumb;
    When sharp winds come
  To flay the hill-tops bleak,
   And whistle down the creek;
    While the unhappy worm
Crawls deeper down into the ground,
To 'scape Frost's jailer on his round;
    Thy form to me shall speak
    From the wide valley's bound,
Recall the waving of the last bird's wing,
    And help me hope for spring.

BEFORE THE SNOW.

Autumn is gone: through the blue woodlands bare
  Shatters the windy rain. A thousand leaves,
Like birds that fly the mournful Northern air,
  Flutter away from the old forest's eaves.

Autumn is gone: as yonder silent rill,
  Slow eddying o'er thick leaf-heaps lately shed,
My spirit, as I walk, moves awed and still,
  By thronging fancies wild and wistful led.

Autumn is gone: alas, how long ago
  The grapes were plucked, and garnered was the grain!
How soon death settles on us, and the snow

Wraps with its white alike our graves, our gain!

Yea, autumn's gone! Yet it robs not my mood
  Of that which makes moods dear, — some shoot of spring
Still sweet within me; or thoughts of yonder wood
  We walked in, — memory's rare environing.

And, though they die, the seasons only take
  A ruined substance. All that's best remains
In the essential vision that can make
  One light for life, love, death, their joys, their pains.

THE GHOSTS OF GROWTH.

Last night it snowed; and Nature fell asleep.
  Forest and field lie tranced in gracious dreams
  Of growth, for ghosts of leaves long dead, me-seems,
Hover about the boughs; and wild winds sweep
O'er whitened fields full many a hoary heap
  From the storm-harvest mown by ice-bound streams!
  With beauty of crushed clouds the cold earth teems,
And winter a tranquil-seeming truce would keep.

But such ethereal slumber may not bide
  The ascending sun's bright scorn — not long, I fear;
And all its visions on the golden tide
  Of mid-noon gliding off, must disappear.
Fair dreams, farewell! So in life's stir and pride
  You fade, and leave the treasure of a tear!

THE LILY-POND.

Some fairy spirit with his wand,
 I think, has hovered o'er the dell,
And spread this film upon the pond,
 And touched it with this drowsy spell.

For here the musing soul is merged
 In moods no other scene can bring,
And sweeter seems the air when scourged
 With wandering wild-bees' murmuring.

One ripple streaks the little lake,
 Sharp purple-blue; the birches, thin
And silvery, crowd the edge, yet break
 To let a straying sunbeam in.

How came we through the yielding wood,
 That day, to this sweet-rustling shore?
Oh, there together while we stood,
 A butterfly was wafted o'er,

In sleepy light; and even now
 His glimmering beauty doth return
Upon me, when the soft winds blow,
 And lilies toward the sunlight yearn.

The yielding wood? And yet 't was both
 To yield unto our happy march;
Doubtful it seemed, at times, if both
 Could pass its green, elastic arch.

Yet there, at last, upon the marge
 We found ourselves, and there, behold,
In hosts the lilies, white and large,

Lay close, with hearts of downy gold!

Deep in the weedy waters spread
  The rootlets of the placid bloom:
So sprung my love's flower, that was bred
  In deep, still waters of heart's-gloom.

So sprung; and so that morn was nursed
  To live in light, and on the pool
Wherein its roots were deep immersed
  Burst into beauty broad and cool.

Few words were said; a moment passed;
  I know not how it came—that awe
And ardor of a glance that cast
  Our love in universal law!

But all at once a bird sang loud,
  From dead twigs of the gleamy beech;
His notes dropped dewy, as out of a cloud,
  A blessing on our married speech.

Ah, Love! how fresh and rare, even now,
  That moment and that mood return
Upon me, when the soft winds blow,
  And lilies toward the sunlight yearn!

PART SECOND.

FIRST GLANCE.

A budding mouth and warm blue eyes;
A laughing face;—and laughing hair,
  So ruddy does it rise
  From off that forehead fair;

Frank fervor in whate'er she said,
And a shy grace when she was still;
  A bright, elastic tread;
  Enthusiastic will;

These wrought the magic of a maid
As sweet and sad as the sun in spring,
  Joyous, yet half-afraid
  Her joyousness to sing.

What weighs the unworthiness of earth
When beauty such as this finds birth?
  Rare maid, to look on thee
  Gives all things harmony!

"THE SUNSHINE OF THINE EYES."

The sunshine of thine eyes,
  (Oh still, celestial beam!)
Whatever it touches it fills
  With the life of its lambent gleam.

The sunshine of thine eyes,
  Oh let it fall on me!
Though I be but a mote of the air,
  I could turn to gold for thee!

"WHEN, LOOKING DEEPLY IN THY FACE."

When, looking deeply in thy face,
I catch the undergleam of grace
That grows beneath the outward glance,
Long looking, lost as in a trance
Of long desires that fleet and meet
Around me like the fresh and sweet
White showers of rain which, vanishing,
'Neath heaven's blue arches whirl, in spring;
Suddenly then I seem to know
Of some new fountain's overflow
In grassy basins, with a sound
That leads my fancy, past all bound,
Into a region of retreat
From this my life's bewildered heat.
Oh if my soul might always draw
From those deep fountains full of awe,
The current of my days should rise
Unto the level of thine eyes!

WITHIN A YEAR

I.

  Lips that are met in love's
    Devotion sweet,
While parting lovers passionately greet,

And earth through heaven's arc more swiftly moves —
    Oh, will they be less dear
    Within a year?

II.

    Eyes in whose shadow-spell
        Far off I read
That which to lovers taking loving heed
Dear women's eyes full soon and plainly tell —
    Oh, will you give such cheer
    This time a year?

III.

    Behold! the dark year goes,
        Nor will reveal
Aught of its purpose, if for woe or weal,
Swift as a stream that o'er the mill-weir flows:
    Mayhap the end draws near
    Within the year!

IV.

    Yet, darling, once more touch
        Those lips to mine.
Set on my life that talisman divine;
Absence, new friends, I fear not overmuch — —
    Even Death, should he appear
    Within the year!

THE SINGING WIRE.

Hark to that faint, ethereal twang
  That from the bosom of the breeze
Has caught its rise and fall: there rang
  Æolian harmonies!

I looked; again the mournful, chords,
  In random rhythm lightly flung
From off the wire, came shaped in words;
  And thus, meseemed, they sung.

"I, messenger of many fates,
  Strung to the tones of woe or weal,
Fine nerve that thrills and palpitates
  With all men know or feel,—

"Oh, is it strange that I should wail?
  Leave me my tearless, sad refrain,
When in the pine-top wakes the gale
  That breathes of coming rain.

"There is a spirit in the post;
  It, too, was once a murmuring tree;
Its sapless, sad, and withered ghost
  Echoes my melody.

"Come close, and lay your listening ear
  Against the bare and branchless wood.
Say, croons it not, so low and clear,
  As if it understood?"

I listened to the branchless pole
  That held aloft the singing wire;
I heard its muffled music roll,

And stirred with sweet desire:

"O wire more soft than seasoned lute,
  Hast thou no sunlit word for me?
Though long to me so coyly mute,
  Sure she may speak through thee!"

I listened; but it was in vain.
  At first, the wind's old, wayward will
Drew forth the tearless, sad refrain:
  That ceased, and all was still.

But suddenly some kindling shock
  Struck flashing through the wire: a bird,
Poised on it, screamed and flew; the flock
  Rose with him, wheeled, and whirred.

Then to my soul there came this sense:
  "Her heart has answered unto thine;
She comes, to-night. Go, hie thee hence!
  Meet her: no more repine!"

Mayhap the fancy was far-fetched;
  And yet, mayhap, it hinted true.
Ere moonrise, Love, a hand was stretched
  In mine, that gave me — you!

And so more dear to me has grown,
  Than rarest tones swept from the lyre,
The minor-movement of that moan
  In yonder singing wire.

Nor care I for the will of states.
  Or aught besides, that smites that string,
Since then so close it knit our fates,

What time the bird took wing!

MOODS OF LOVE.

I.

IN ABSENCE.

My love for thee is like a winged seed
  Blown from the heart of thy rare beauty's flower,
  And deftly guided by some breezy power
To fall and rest, where I should never heed,
In deepest caves of memory. There, indeed,
  With virtue rife of many a sunny hoar,—
  Ev'n making cold neglect and darkness dower
Its roots with life,—swiftly it 'gan to breed,
Till now wide-branching tendrils it outspreads
  Like circling arms, to prison its own prison,
Fretting the walls with blooms by myriads,
  And blazoning in my brain full summer-season:
Thy face, whose dearness presence had not taught.
In absence multiplies, and fills all thought.

II.

HEART'S FOUNTAIN.

Her moods are like the fountain's, changing ever,
  That spouts aloft a sudden, watery dome,
  Only to fall again in shattering foam,
Just where the wedded jets themselves dissever,
And palpitating downward, downward quiver,
  Unfolded like a swift ethereal flower,

That sheds white petals in a blinding shower,
And straightway soars anew with blithe endeavor.

The sun may kindle it with healthful fire;
  Upon it falls the cloud-gray's leaden load;
At night the stars shall haunt the whirling spire:
  Yet these have but a transient garb bestowed.
So her glad life, whate'er the hours impart,
Plays still 'twixt heaven's cope and her own clear heart.

III.

SOUTH-WIND SONG.

Soft-throated South, breathing of summer's ease
  (Sweet breath, whereof the violet's life is made!)
  Through lips moist-warm, as thou hadst lately stayed
'Mong rosebuds, wooing to the cheeks of these
Loth blushes faint and maidenly — rich Breeze,
  Still doth thy honeyed blowing bring a shade
  Of sad foreboding. In thy hand is laid
The power to build or blight rich fruit of trees,
The deep, cool grass, and field of thick-combed grain.

Even so my Love may bring me joy or woe,
  Both measureless, but either counted gain
Since given by her. For pain and pleasure flow
  Like tides upon us of the self-same sea.
  Tears are the gems of joy and misery!

IV.

THE LOVER'S YEAR

Thou art my morning, twilight, noon, and eve,
  My Summer and my Winter, Spring and Fall;
  For Nature left on thee a touch of all
The moods that come to gladden or to grieve
The heart of Time, with purpose to relieve
  From lagging sameness. So do these forestall
  In thee such o'erheaped sweetnesses as pall
Too swiftly, and the taster tasteless leave.

Scenes that I love to me always remain
  Beautiful, whether under summer's sun
Beheld, or, storm-dark, stricken across with rain.
  So, through all humors, thou 'rt the same sweet one:
Doubt not I love thee well in each, who see
Thy constant change is changeful constancy.

V.

NEW WORLDS.

With my beloved I lingered late one night.
  At last the hour when I must leave her came:
  But, as I turned, a fear I could not name
Possessed me that the long sweet evening might
Prelude some sudden storm, whereby delight
  Should perish. What if Death, ere dawn, should claim
  One of us? What, though living, not the same
Each should appear to each in morning-light?

Changed did I find her, truly, the next day:
  Ne'er could I see her as of old again.
That strange mood seemed to draw a cloud away,
  And let her beauty pour through every vein

Sunlight and life, part of me. Thus the lover
With each new morn a new world may discover.

VI.

WEDDING-NIGHT.

At night, with shaded eyes, the summer moon
  In tender meditation downward glances
  At the dark earth, far-set in dim expanses,
And, welcomer than blazoned gold of noon,
Down through the air her steady lights are strewn.
  The breezy forests sigh in moonlit trances,
  And the full-hearted poet, waking, fancies
The smiling hills will break in laughter soon.

Oh thus, thou gentle Nature, dost thou shine
  On me to-night. My very limbs would melt,
Like rugged earth beneath yon ray divine,
  Into faint semblance of what they have felt:
Thine eye doth color me, O wife, O mine,
With peace that in thy spirit long hath dwelt!

LOVE'S DEFEAT.

A thousand times I would have hoped,
  A thousand times protested;
But still, as through the night I groped,
  My torch from me was wrested,
      and wrested.

How often with a succoring cup
  Unto the hurt I hasted!

The wounded died ere I came up;
  My cup was still untasted, —
    Untasted.

Of darkness, wounds, and harsh disdain
  Endured, I ne'er repented.
'T is not of these I would complain:
  With these I were contented, —
    Contented.

Here lies the misery, to feel
  No work of love completed;
In prayerless passion still to kneel,
  And mourn, and cry: "Defeated
    Defeated!"

MAY AND MARRIAGE.

THE LOVER WHO THINKS.

Dost thou remember, Love, those hours
Shot o'er with random rainy showers,
When the bold sun would woo coy May?
She smiled, then wept—and looked another way.

We, learning from the sun and season,
Together plotted joyous treason
'Gainst maiden majesty, to give
Each other troth, and henceforth wedded live.

But love, ah, love we know is blind!
Not always what they seek they find
When, groping through dim-lighted natures,
Fond lovers look for old, ideal statures.

What then? Is all our purpose lost?
The balance broken, since Fate tossed
Uneven weights? Oh well beware
That thought, my sweet: 't were neither fit nor fair!

Seek not for any grafted fruits
From souls so wedded at the roots;
But whatsoe'er our fibres hold,
Let that grow forth in mutual, ample mold!

No sap can circle without flaw
Into the perfect sphere we saw
Hanging before our happy eyes

Amid the shade of marriage-mysteries;

But all that in the heart doth lurk
Must toward the mystic shaping work:
Sweet fruit and bitter both must fall
When the boughs bend, at each year's autumn-call.

Ah, dear defect! that aye shall lift
Us higher, not through craven shift
Of fault on common frailty;—nay,
But twofold hope to help with generous stay!

I shall be nearer, understood:
More prized art thou than perfect good.
And since thou lov'st me, I shall grow
Thy other self—thy Life, thy Joy, thy Woe!

THE FISHER OF THE CAPE.

At morn his bark like a bird
Slips lightly oceanward—
Sail feathering smooth o'er the bay
And beak that drinks the wild spray.
In his eyes beams cheerily
A light like the sun's on the sea,
As he watches the waning strand,
Where the foam, like a waving hand
Of one who mutely would tell
Her love, flutters faintly, "Farewell."

But at night, when the winds arise
And pipe to driving skies,
And the moon peers, half afraid,
Through the storm-cloud's ragged shade,

He hears her voice in the blast
That sighs about the mast,
He sees her face in the clouds
As he climbs the whistling shrouds;
And a power nerves his hand,
Shall bring the bark to land.

SAILOR'S SONG.

The sea goes up; the sky comes down.
Oh, can you spy the ancient town, —
The granite hills so hard and gray,
That rib the land behind the bay?
　O ye ho, boys! Spread her wings!
　Fair winds, boys: send her home!
　　O ye ho!

Three years? Is it so long that we
Have lived upon the lonely sea?
Oh, often I thought we'd see the town,
When the sea went up, and the sky came down.
　O ye ho, boys! Spread her wings!
　Fair winds, boys: send her home!
　　O ye ho!

Even the winter winds would rouse
A memory of my father's house;
For round his windows and his door
They made the same deep, mouthless roar.
　O ye ho, boys! Spread her wings!
　Fair winds, boys: send her home!
　　O ye ho!

And when the summer's breezes beat,
Methought I saw the sunny street
Where stood my Kate. Beneath her hand
She gazed far out, far out from land.
  O ye ho, boys! Spread her wings!
  Fair winds, boys: send her home!
    O ye ho!

Farthest away, I oftenest dreamed
That I was with her. Then, it seemed
A single stride the ocean wide
Had bridged, and brought me to her side.
  O ye ho, boys! Spread her wings!
  Fair winds, boys: send her home.
    O ye ho!

But though so near we're drawing, now,
'T is farther off — —I know not how.
We sail and sail: we see no home.
Would we into the port were come!
  O ye ho, boys! Spread her wings!
  Fair winds, boys: send her home!
    O ye ho!

At night, the same stars o'er the mast:
The mast sways round — however fast
We fly — still sways and swings around
One scanty circle's starry bound.
  O ye ho, boys! Spread her wings!
  Fair winds, boys: send her home!
    O ye ho!

Ah, many a month those stars have shone,
And many a golden morn has flown,
Since that so solemn, happy morn,
When, I away, my babe was born.
  O ye ho, boys! Spread her wings!

Fair winds, boys: send her home!
  O ye ho!

And, though so near we're drawing, now,
'T is farther off—I know not how—
I would not aught amiss had come
To babe or mother there, at home!
  O ye ho, boys! Spread her wings!
  Fair winds, boys: send her home!
    O ye ho!

'T is but a seeming: swiftly rush
The seas, beneath. I hear the crush
Of foamy ridges 'gainst the prow.
Longing outspeeds the breeze, I know.
  O ye ho, boys! Spread her wings!
  Fair winds, boys: send her home!
    O ye ho!

Patience, my mates! Though not this eve
We cast our anchor, yet believe,
If but the wind holds, short the run:
We 'll sail in with to-morrow's sun.
  O ye ho, boys! Spread her wings!
  Fair winds, boys: send her home!
    O ye ho!

JESSAMINE.

Here stands the great tree still, with broad, bent head,
And wide arms grown aweary, yet outspread
With their old blessing. But wan memory weaves
Strange garlands now amongst the darkening leaves.

And the moon hangs low in the elm.

Beneath these glimmering arches Jessamine
Walked with her lover long ago, and in
This moon-made shade he questioned; and she spoke:
Then on them both love's rarer radiance broke.
And the moon hangs low in the elm.

Sweet Jessamine we called her; for she shone
Like blossoms that in sun and shade have grown,
Gathering from each alike a perfect white,
Whose rich bloom breaks opaque through darkest night.
And the moon hangs low in the elm.

And for this sweetness Walt, her lover, sought
To win her; wooed her here, his heart full-fraught
With fragrance of her being, and gained his plea.
So "We will wed," they said, "beneath this tree."
And the moon hangs low in the elm.

Was it unfaith, or faith more full to her,
Made him, for fame and fortune longing, spur
Into the world? Far from his home he sailed:
And life paused; while she watched joy vanish, vailed.
And the moon hangs low in the elm.

Oh, better at the elm tree's sun-browned feet
If he had been content to let life fleet
Its wonted way!—there rearing his small house;
Mowing and milking, lord of corn and cows!
And the moon hangs low in the elm.

For as against a snarling sea one steers,
Ever he battled with the beetling years;
And ever Jessamine must watch and pine,
Her vision bounded by the bleak sea-line.

And the moon hangs low in the elm.

At last she heard no more. The neighbors said
That Walt had married, faithless, or was dead.
Yet naught her trust could move; the tryst she kept
Each night still, 'neath this tree, before she slept.
And the moon hangs low in the elm.

So, circling years went by; and in her face
Slow melancholy wrought a tempered grace
Of early joy with sorrow's rich alloy —
Refinèd, rare, no doom should e'er destroy.
And the moon hangs low in the elm.

Sometimes at twilight, when sweet Jessamine,
Slow-footed, weary-eyed, passed by to win
The elm, we smiled for pity of her, and mused
On love that so could live with love refused.
And the moon hangs low in the elm.

Nor none could hope for her. But she had grown
Too high in love for hope, and bloomed alone,
Aloft in pure sincerity secure;
For fortune's failures, in her faith too sure.
And the moon hangs low in the elm.

Oh, well for Walt, if he had known her soul!
Discouraged on disaster's changeful shoal
Wrecking, he rested; starved on selfish pride
Long years; nor would obey love's homeward tide.
And the moon hangs low in the elm.

But, bitterly repenting of his sin,
Oh, bitterly he learned to look within
Sweet Jessamine's clear depth — when the past, dead,
Mocked him, and wild, waste years forever fled!

And the moon hangs low in the elm.

Late, late, oh, late beneath the tree stood two!
In awe and anguish wondering: "Is it true?"
Two that were each most like to some wan wraith:
Yet each on each looked with a living faith.
And the moon hangs low in the elm.

Even to the tree-top sang the wedding-bell;
Even to the tree-top tolled the passing knell.
Beneath it Walt and Jessamine were wed;
Beneath it many a year she lieth dead!
And the moon hangs low in the elm.

Here stands the great tree still. But age has crept
Through every coil, while Walt each night has kept
The tryst alone. Hark! with what windy might
The boughs chant o'er her grave their burial-rite!
And the moon hangs low in the elm.

GRIEF'S HERO.

A youth unto herself Grief took,
Whom everything of joy forsook,
And men passed with denying head,
Saying: "'T were better he were dead."

Grief took him, and with master-touch
Molded his being. I marveled much
To see her magic with the clay,
So much she gave—and took away.
Daily she wrought, and her design
Grew daily clearer and more fine,
To make the beauty of his shape

Serve for the spirit's free escape.
With liquid fire she filled his eyes.
She graced his lips with swift surmise
Of sympathy for others' woe,
And made his every fibre flow
In fairer curves. On brow and chin
And tinted cheek, drawn clean and thin,
She sculptured records rich, great Grief!
She made him loving, made him lief.

I marveled; for, where others saw
A failing frame with many a flaw,
Meseemed a figure I beheld
Fairer than anything of eld
Fashioned from sunny marble. Here
Nature was artist with no peer.
No chisel's purpose could have caught
These lines, nor brush their secret wrought.
Not so the world weighed, busily
Pursuing drossy industry;
But, saturated with success,
Well-guarded by a soft excess
Of bodily ease, gave little heed
To him that held not by their creed,
Save o'er the beauteous youth to moan:
"A pity that he is not grown
To our good stature and heavier weight,
To bear his share of our full freight."
Meanwhile, thus to himself he spoke:
"Oh, noble is the knotted oak,
And sweet the gush of sylvan streams,
And good the great sun's gladding beams,
The blush of life upon the field,
The silent might that mountains wield.
Still more I love to mix with men,
Meeting the kindly human ken;
To feel the force of faithful friends —

The thirst for smiles that never ends.

"Yet precious more than all of these
I hold great Sorrow's mysteries,
Whereby Gehenna's sultry gale
Is made to lift the golden veil
'Twixt heaven's starry-spherèd light
Of truth and our dim, sun-blent sight.
Joy comes to ripen; but 'tis Grief
That garners in the grainy sheaf.
Time was I feared to know or feel
The spur of aught but gilded weal;
To bear aloft the victor, Fame,
Would ev'n have champed a stately shame
Of bit and bridle. But my fears
Fell off in the pure bath of tears.
And now with sinews fresh and strong
I stride, to summon with a song
The deep, invigorating truth
That makes me younger than my youth.
"O Sorrow, deathless thy delight!
Deathless it were but for our slight
Endurance! Truth like thine, too rare,
We dare but take in scantiest share."

He died: the creatures of his kind
Fared on. Not one had known his mind.

But the unnamed yearnings of the air,
The eternal sky's wide-searching stare,
The undertone of brawling floods,
And the old moaning of the woods
Grew full of memory.

      The sun
Many a brave heart has shone upon
Since then, of men who walked abroad

For joy and gladness praising God.
But widowed Grief lives on alone:
She hath not chosen, of them, one.

A FACE IN THE STREET.

Poor, withered face, that yet was once so fair,
  Grown ashen-old in the wild fires of lust—
  Thy star-like beauty, dimm'd with earthly dust,
  Yet breathing of a purer native air;—
They who whilom, cursed vultures, sought a share
  Of thy dead womanhood, their greed unjust
  Have satisfied, have stripped and left thee bare.
  Still, like a leaf warped by the autumn gust,
And driving to the end, thou wrapp'st in flame
  And perfume all thy hollow-eyed decay,
Feigning on those gray cheeks the blush that Shame
  Took with her when she fled long since away.
    Ah God! rain fire upon this foul-souled city
    That gives such death, and spares its men,—for pity!

THE BATHER.

Standing here alone,
Let me pause awhile,
Drinking in the light
Ere, with plunge of white limbs prone,
I raise the sparkling flight
Of foam-flakes volatile.

Now, in natural guise,
I woo the deathless breeze,
Through me rushing fleet

The joy of life, in swift surprise:
I grow with growing wheat,
And burgeon with the trees.

Lo! I fetter Time,
So he cannot run;
And in Eden again—
Flash of memory sublime!—
Dwell naked, without stain,
Beneath the dazed sun.

All yields brotherhood;
Each least thing that lives,
Wrought of primal spores,
Deepens this wild sense of good
That, on these shaggy shores,
Return to nature gives.

Oh, that some solitude
Were ours, in woodlands deep,
Where, with lucent eyes,
Living lithe and limber-thewed,
Our life's shape might arise
Like mountains fresh from sleep!

To sounds of water falling,
Hosts of delicate dreams
Should lull us and allure
With a dim, enchanted calling,
Blameless to live and pure
Like these sweet springs and streams.

But in a wilderness
Alone may such life be?
Why of all things framed,
In my human form confessed

Should I be ashamed,
And blush for honesty?

Rounded, strengthy limbs
That knit me to my kind —
Your glory turns to grief!
Shall I for my soul sing hymns,
Yet for my body find
No clear, divine belief?

Let me rather die,
Than by faith uphold
Dogmas weak that dare
The form that once Christ wore deny
Afraid with him to share
A purity twofold;

Yet, while sin remains
On this saddened earth,
Humbly walk my ways!
For my garments are as chains;
And I fear to praise
My frame with careless mirth.

Joy and penance go
Hand in hand, I see!
Would I could live so well,
Soul of me should never know
When my coverings fell,
Nor feel this nudity!

HELEN AT THE LOOM.

Helen, in her silent room,
Weaves upon the upright loom,
Weaves a mantle rich and dark,
Purpled over-deep. But mark
How she scatters o'er the wool
Woven shapes, till it is full
Of men that struggle close, complex;
Short-clipp'd steeds with wrinkled necks
Arching high; spear, shield, and all
The panoply that doth recall
Mighty war, such war as e'en
For Helen's sake is waged, I ween.
Purple is the groundwork: good!
All the field is stained with blood.
Blood poured out for Helen's sake;
(Thread, run on; and, shuttle, shake!)
But the shapes of men that pass
Are as ghosts within a glass,
Woven with whiteness of the swan,
Pale, sad memories, gleaming wan
From the garment's purple fold
Where Troy's tale is twined and told.
Well may Helen, as with tender
Touch of rosy fingers slender
She doth knit the story in
Of Troy's sorrow and her sin,
Feel sharp filaments of pain
Reeled off with the well-spun skein,
And faint blood-stains on her hands
From the shifting sanguine strands.
Gently, sweetly she doth sorrow:
What has been must be to-morrow;
Meekly to her fate she bows.
Heavenly beauties still will rouse
Strife and savagery in men:
Shall the lucid heavens, then,
Lose their high serenity,

Sorrowing over what must be?
If she taketh to her shame,
Lo, they give her not the blame, —
Priam's wisest counselors,
Aged men, not loving wars:
When she goes forth, clad in white,
Day-cloud touched by first moonlight,
With her fair hair, amber-hued
As vapor by the moon imbued
With burning brown, that round her clings,
See, she sudden silence brings
On the gloomy whisperers
Who would make the wrong all hers.

So, Helen, in thy silent room,
Labor at the storied loom;
(Thread, run on; and, shuttle, shake!)
Let thy aching sorrow make
Something strangely beautiful
Of this fabric, since the wool
Comes so tinted from the Fates,
Dyed with loves, hopes, fears, and hates.
Thou shalt work with subtle force
All thy deep shade of remorse
In the texture of the weft,
That no stain on thee be left; —
Ay, false queen, shalt fashion grief,
Grief and wrong, to soft relief.
Speed the garment! It may chance.
Long hereafter, meet the glance
Of none; when her lord,
Now thy Paris, shall go t'ward
Ida, at his last sad end,
Seeking her, his early friend,
Who alone can cure his ill
Of all who love him, if she will.
It were fitting she should see
In that hour thine artistry,

And her husband's speechless corse
In the garment of remorse!
But take heed that in thy work
Naught unbeautiful may lurk.
Ah, how little signifies
Unto thee what fortunes rise,
What others fall! Thou still shalt rule,
Still shalt work the colored crewl.
Though thy yearning woman's eyes
Burn with glorious agonies,
Pitying the waste and woe,
And the heroes falling low
In the war around thee, here,
Yet that exquisitest tear
'Twixt thy lids shall dearer be
Than life, to friend or enemy.

There are people on the earth
Doomed with doom of too great worth.
Look on Helen not with hate,
Therefore, but compassionate.
If she suffer not too much,
Seldom does she feel the touch
Of that fresh, auroral joy
Lighter spirits may decoy
To their pure and sunny lives.
Heavy honey 't is, she hives.
To her sweet but burdened soul
All that here she doth control —
What of bitter memories,
What of coming fate's surmise,
Paris' passion, distant din
Of the war now drifting in
To her quiet — idle seems;
Idle as the lazy gleams
Of some stilly water's reach,
Seen from where broad vine-leaves pleach
A heavy arch, and, looking through,

Far away the doubtful blue
Glimmers, on a drowsy day,
Crowded with the sun's rich gray,
As she stands within her room,
Weaving, weaving at the loom.

"O WHOLESOME DEATH."

O Wholesome Death, thy sombre funeral-car
  Looms ever dimly on the lengthening way
  Of life; while, lengthening still, in sad array,
My deeds in long procession go, that are
As mourners of the man they helped to mar.
  I see it all in dreams, such as waylay
  The wandering fancy when the solid day
Has fallen in smoldering ruins, and night's star,
Aloft there, with its steady point of light
  Mastering the eye, has wrapped the brain in sleep.
Ah, when I die, and planets take their flight
  Above my grave, still let my spirit keep
Sometimes its vigil of divine remorse,
'Midst pity, praise, or blame heaped o'er my corse!

BURIAL-SONG FOR SUMNER.

    Now the last wreath of snow
    That melts, in mist exhales
White aspiration, and our deep-voiced gales
In chorus chant the measured march of spring,
    Whom griefs of life and death
      Are burdening!
        Slow, slow —
      With half-held breath —

Tread slow, O mourners, that all men may know
    What hero here lies low!

    O music, sweep
    From some deep cave, and bear
To us that gasp in this so meagre air
    Sweet ministerings
And consolations of contorted sound,
    With agonies profound
Of nobly warring and enduring chords
    That lie, close-bound,
Unstirred as yet 'neath thy wide, wakening wings;
So that our hearts break not in broken words.
    O music, that hast power
    This darkness to devour
In vivid light; that from the dusk of grief
Canst cause to grow divergent flower and leaf,
    And from death's darkest roots
    Bring forth the fairest fruits;—
    Come thou, to quicken this hour
    Of loss, and keep
Thy spell on all, that none may dare to weep!

    For he whom now we mourn,
    As if from giants born,
Was strong in limb and strong in brain,
And nobly with a giant scorn
    Withstood the direst pain
    That healing science knows,
    When, by the dastard blows
    Of his brute enemy
Laid low, he sought to rise again
    Through help of knife and fire,—
    The awful enginery
    Wherewith men dare aspire
To wrest from Death his victims. Yea,
Though he who healed him shrank and throbbed
    With horror of the wound,

Brave Sumner gave no sound,
Nor flinched, nor sobbed,
But as though within the man
Instant premonition ran
    Of his high fate,
Imperishable, sculptured state
    Enthroned in death to hold,
    He stood, a statued form
    Of veiled and voiceless storm,
    Inwardly quivering
    Like the swift-smitten string
    Of unheard music, yet
    As massively and firmly set
As if he had been marble or wrought gold!

    Built in so brave a shape,
    How could he hope escape
    The blundering people's wrath?
        Who, seeing him strong,
Supposed it right to cast on him their wrong,
    Since he could bear it all!
    Lo, now, the sombre pall
  Sweeps their dull errors from the path,
        And leaves it free
For him, whose hushed heart no reproaches hath,
    Unto his grave to fare,
    In shrouded majesty!
    His triumph fills the air:
Behold, the streets are bordered with vain breath
Of those who reverent watch the train of death;
    But he has done with breathing!

    Wise Death, still choosing near and far,
    Thou couldst not strike a higher star
    From out our heaven, and yet its light
    In falling glorifies the night!

Leader in life, his lips, though dumb,
Still rule us by their restfulness, their smile
Of far-off meanings; and the people come
In tributary hosts for many a mile,
    Drawn by an eloquence
    More solemn and intense
    Than that wherewith he shook
    The Senate, while his look
Of sober lightning cleft the knotty growth
Of error, that within the riven root
Uplifted, lit with peace, truth's buds might shoot,
And blow sweet breath o'er all, however loth!

Unspeaking, though his eyes forget
  The light that late forsook
  Their chambers, there doth rise
    Mysteriously yet
  A radiance thence that glows
On brows of them, the great and wise,
Poets and men of prophecies,
Who, with looks of strange repose,
Calm, exalted, here have met
Him to follow to his grave.
Well they know he's crossed their bound,
Yet, with baffled longing brave,
Seek with him the depths to sound
That gulf our lonely life around.
Oh, on these mortal faces frail
  What immortality
  Falls from the death-light pale!

Ev'n thus the path unto thy tomb,
Sumner, all our brave and good
Still shall pace through time to come,
For in distant Auburn wood
Seeing the glimmer of thy stone,
They a shaft shall deem it, thrown
From a dawn beyond the deep,

And so haste with thee to keep
   Angelic brotherhood!
   O herald, gone before,
   For these throw wide the door,
   Make room, make room!

   Now, music, cease,
And bitter brazen trumpets hold your peace!
   Now, while the dumb, white air
   Draws from our still despair
      A purer prayer.
      Then must the sod
   Fulfill its humble share,
   Meek-folded o'er his breast,
Here where he lies amongst the waiting trees:
They shall break bud when warm winds from the west
And southern breezes come to touch the place
      Made precious by this grace
      Of memory dear to God.

We leave him where the granite Lion lies
And gazes toward the East, with woman's eyes
That read the riddle of the undying sun,
Bearing within her breast the stony germ
Of continents, but—lasting no less firm—
      The memory of those marvels done,
      The battles fought, the words that wrought
      To free a race, and chasten one.
We leave him where the river slowly winds,
      A broken chain;
The river that so late its hero finds,
      Without a stain,
Whose name so long expectantly it bore;
   And, echoing now a people's thought,
The Charles shall murmur by this reedy shore
      His fame forevermore.

ARISE, AMERICAN!

The soul of a nation awaking, —
  High visions of daybreak I saw,
And the stir of a state, the forsaking
  Of sin, and the worship of law.

O pine-tree, shout! And hoarser
  Rush, river, unto the sea,
Foam-fettered and sun-flushed, a courser
  That feels the prairie, free!

Our birth-star beckons to trial
  All faith of the far-fled years,
Ere scorn was our share, and denial,
  Or laughter for patriot's tears.

And lo, Faith comes forth the finer
  From trampled thickets of fire,
And the orient opens diviner
  Before her; the heaven lifts higher.

O deep, sweet eyes, and severer
  Than steel! he knoweth who comes,
Thy hero: bend thine eyes nearer!
  Now wilder than battle-drums

Thy glance in his blood is stirring!
  His heart is alive like the main
When the roweled winds are spurring,
  And the broad tides shoreward strain.

O hero, art thou among us?
  O helper, hidest thou still?
Why hath he no anthem sung us,

Why waiteth, nor worketh our will?

For still a smirk or a favor
  Can hide the face of the false;
And the old-time Faith seeks braver
  Upholders, and sacreder walls.

Yea, cunning is Christian evil,
  And subtle the conscience' snare;
But virtue's volcanic upheaval
  Shall cast fine device to the air!

Too long has the land's soul slumbered,
  And triumph bred dangerous ease, —
Our victories all unnumbered,
  Our feet on the down-bowed seas.

Come, then, simple and stalwart
  Life of the earlier days!
Come! Far better than all were it —
  Our precepts, our prayers, and our lays —

That the heart of the people should tremble
  Accord to some mighty one's voice,
The helpless atoms assemble
  In music, their valor to poise.

Come to us, mountain-dweller,
  Leader, wherever thou art,
Skilled from thy cradle, a queller
  Of serpents, and sound to the heart!

Modest, and mighty, and tender,
  Man of an iron mold,
Learned or unlearned, our defender,

American-souled!

THE SILENT TIDE

A tangled orchard round the farm-house spreads,
Wherein it stands home-like, but desolate,
'Midst crowded and uneven-statured sheds,
Alike by rain and sunshine sadly stained.
A quiet country-road before the door
Runs, gathering close its ruts to scale the hill—
A sudden bluff on the New Hampshire coast,
That rises rough against the sea, and hangs
Crested above the bowlder-sprinkled beach.
And on the road white houses small are strung
Like threaded beads, with intervals. The church
Tops the rough hill; then comes the wheelwright's shop.

From orchard, church, and shop you hear the sea,
And from the farm-house windows see it strike
Sharp gleams through slender arching apple-boughs.

Sea-like, too, echoing round me here there rolls
A surging sorrow; and even so there breaks
A smitten light of woe upon me, now,
Seeing this place, and telling o'er again
The tale of those who dwelt here once. Long since
It was, and they were two—two brothers, bound
By early orphanage and solitude
The closer, cleaving strongly each to each,
Till love, that held them many years in gage,
Itself swept them asunder. I have heard
The story from old Deacon Snow, their friend,
He who was boy and man with them. A boy!
What, he? How strange it seems! who now is stiff
And warped with life's fierce heat and cold: his brows

Are hoary white, and on his head the hairs
Stand sparse as wheat-stalks on the bare field's edge!

Reuben and Jerry they were named; but two
Of common blood and nurture scarce were found
More sharply different. For the first was bold,
Breeze-like and bold to come or go; not rash,
But shrewdly generous, popular, and boon:
And Jerry, dark and sad-faced. Whether least
He loved himself or neighbor none could tell,
So cold he seemed in wonted sympathy.
Yet he would ponder an hour at a time
Upon a bird found dead; and much he loved
To brood i' th' shade of yon wind-wavered pines.
Often at night, too, he would wander forth,
Lured by the hollow rumbling of the sea
In moonlight breaking, there to learn wild things,
Such as these dreamers pluck out of the dusk
While other men lie sleeping. But a star,
Rose on his sight, at last, with power to rule
Majestically mild that deep-domed sky,
High as youth's hopes, that stood above his soul;
And, ruling, led him dayward. That was Grace,
I mean Grace Brierly, daughter of the squire,
Rivaling the wheelwright Hungerford's shy Ruth
For beauty. Therefore, in the sunny field,
Mowing the clover-purpled grass, or, waked
In keen December dawns, — while creeping light
And winter-tides beneath the pallid stars
Stole o'er the marsh together, — a thought of her
Would turn him cool or warm, like the south breeze,
And make him blithe or bitter. Alas for him!
Eagerly storing golden thoughts of her,
He locked a phantom treasure in his breast.

He sought to chain the breezes, and to lift
A perfume as a pearl before his eyes —
Intangible delight! A time drew on

When from these twilight musings on his hopes
He woke, and found the morning of his love
Blasted, and all its rays shorn suddenly.
For Reuben, too, had turned his eye on Grace,
And she with favoring face the suit had met,
Known in the village; this dream-fettered youth
Perceiving not what passed, until too late.

One holiday the young folks all had gone
Strawberrying, with the village Sabbath-school;
Reuben and Grace and Jerry, Ruth, Rob Snow,
And all their friends, youth-mates that buoyantly
Bore out 'gainst Time's armadas, like a fleet
Of fair ships, sunlit, braced by buffeting winds,
Indomitably brave; but, soon or late,
Battle and hurricane or whirl them deep
Below to death, or send them homeward, seared
By shot and storm: so went they forth, that day.

Two wagons full of rosy children rolled
Along the rutty track, 'twixt swamp and slope,
Through deep, green-glimmering woods, and out at last
On grassy table-land, warm with the sun
And yielding tributary odors wild
Of strawberry, late June-rose, juniper,
Where sea and land breeze mingled. There a brook
Through a bare hollow flashing, spurted, purled,
And shot away, yet stayed—a light and grace
Unconscious and unceasing. And thick pines,
Hard by, drew darkly far away their dim
And sheltering, cool arcades. So all dismount,
And fields and forest gladden with their shout;
Ball, swing, and see-saw sending the light hearts
Of the children high o'er earth and everything.
While some staid, kindly women draw and spread
In pine-shade the long whiteness of a cloth,
The rest, a busy legion, o'er the grass

Kneeling, must rifle the meadow of its fruit.

O laughing Fate! O treachery of truth
To royal hopes youth bows before! That day,
Ev'n there where life in such glad measure beat
Its round, with winds and waters, tunefully,
And birds made music in the matted wood,
The shaft of death reached Jerry's heart: he saw
The sweet conspiracy of those two lives,
In looks and gestures read his doom, and heard
Their laughter ring to the grave all mirth of his.

So Reuben's life in full leaf stood, its fruit
Hidden in a green expectancy; but all
His days were rounded with ripe consciousness:
While Jerry felt the winter's whitening blight,
As when that frosty fern-work and those palms
Of visionary leaf, and trailing vines,
Quaint-chased by night-winds on the pane, melt off,
And naked earth, stone-stiff, with bristling trees,
Stares in the winter sunlight coldly through.
But yet he rose, and clothed himself amain
With misery, and once more put on life
As a stained garment. Highly he resolved
To make his deedless days henceforward strike
Pure harmony — a psalm of silences.

But on the Sunday, coming from the church,
He saw those happy, plighted lovers walk
Before proud Grace's father, and of friends
Heard comment and congratulation given.
Then with Rob Snow he hurried to the beach,
To a rough heap of stones they two had reared
In boyhood. There the two held sad debate
Of life's swift losses, Bob inspiriting still,
Jerry rejecting hope, ev'n though his friend,
Self-wounding (for he loved Ruth Hungerford),

Told how the wheelwright's daughter longed for him,
And yet might make him glad, though Grace was lost.

The season deepened, and in Jerry's heart
Ripened a thought charged with grave consequence.
His grief he would have stifled at its birth,
Sad child of frustrate longing! But anon—
Knowledge of Ruth's affection being revealed,
Which, if he stayed to let it feed on him,
Vine-like might wreathe and wind about his life,
Lifting all shade and sweetness out of reach
Of Robert, so long his friend—honor, and hopes
He would not name, kindled a torch for war
Of various impulse in him. Reuben wedded;
Yet Jerry lingered. Then, swift whisperings
Along reverberant walls of gossips' ears
Hummed loud and louder a love for Ruth. Grace, too,
Involved him in a web of soft surmise
With Ruth; and Reuben questioned him thereof.
But a white, sudden anger struck like a bolt
O'er Jerry's face, that blackened under it:
He strode away, and left his brother dazed,
With red rush of offended self-conceit
Staining his forehead to the hair. This flash
Of anger—first since boyhood's wholesome strifes—
On Jerry's path gleamed lurid; by its light
He shaped a life's course out.

              There came a storm
One night. He bade farewell to Ruth; and when
Above the seas the bare-browed dawn arose,
While the last laggard drops ran off the eaves,
He dressed, but took some customary garb
On his arm; stole swiftly to the sands; and there
Cast clown his garments by the ancient heap
Of stones. At first brief pause he made, and thought:
"And thus I play, to win perchance a tear
From her whom, first, to save the smallest care,

I thought I could have died!" But then at once
Within the sweep of swirling water-planes
That from the great waves circled up and slid
Instantly back, passing far down the shore,
Southward he made his way. Next day he shipped
Upon a whaler outward bound. She spread
Her mighty wings, and bore him far away —
So far, Death seemed across her wake to stalk,
Withering her swift shape from the empty air,
Until her memory grew a faded dream.

Ah, what a desolate brightness that young day
Flung o'er the impassive strand and dull green marsh
And green-arched orchard, ere it struck the farm!
Storm-strengthened, clear, and cool the morning rose
To gaze down on that frighted home, where dawned
Pale Ruth's discovery of her loss, who late,
Guessing some ill in Jerry's last-night words
Of vague farewell, woke now to certainty
Of strange disaster. So, when Reuben and Rob,
Hither and thither searching, with locked lips
And eyes grown suddenly cold in eager dread,
On those still sands beside the untamed sea,
Came to the garments Jerry had thrown there, dumb
They stood, and knew he'd perished. If by chance
Borne out with undertow and rolled beneath
The gaping surge, or rushing on his death
Free-willed, they would not guess; but straight they set
Themselves to watch the changes of the sea —
The watchful sea that would not be betrayed,
The surly flood that echoed their suspense
With hollow-sounding horror. Thus three tides
Hurled on the beach their empty spray, and brought
Nor doubt-dispelling death, nor new-born hope.
But with the fourth slow turn at length there came
A naked, drifting body impelled to shore,
An unknown sailor by the late storm swept
Out of the rigging of some laboring ship.

And him, disfigured by the water's wear,
The watching friends supposed their dead; and so,
Mourning, took up this outcast of the deep,
And buried him, with church-rite and with pall
Trailing, and train of sad-eyed mourners, there
In the old orchard-lot by Reuben's door.

Observed among the mourners walked slight Ruth.
Her grief had dropped a veil of finer light
Around her, hedging her with sanctity
Peculiar; all stood shy about her save
Rob Snow, he venturing from time to time
Some small, uncertain act of kindliness.
Long seemed she vowed from joy, but when the birds
Began to mate, and quiet violets blow
Along the brook-side, lo! she smiled again;
Again the wind-flower color in her cheeks
Blanch'd in a breath, and bloomed once more; then stayed;
Till, like the breeze that rumors ripening buds,
A delicate sense crept through the air that soon
These two would scale the church-crowned hill, and wed.

The seasons faced the world, and fled, and came.
In summer nights, the soft roll of the sea
Was shattered, resonant, beneath a moon
That, silent, seemed to hearken. And every hour
In autumn, night or day, large apples fell
Without rebound to earth, upon the sod
There mounded greenly by the large slate slab
In the old orchard-lot near Reuben's door.
But there were changes: after some long years
Reuben and Grace beheld a brave young boy
Bearing their double life abroad in one —
Beginning new the world, and bringing hopes
That in their path fell flower-like. Not at ease
They dwelt, though; for a slow discordancy
Of temper — weak-willed waste of life in bursts
Of petulance — had marred their happiness.

And so the boy, young Reuben, as he grew,
Was chafed and vexed by this ill-fitting mode
Of life forced on him, and rebelled. Too oft
Brooding alone, he shaped loose schemes of flight
Into the joyous outer world, to break
From the unwholesome wranglings of his home.
Then once, when at some slight demur he made,
Dispute ensued between the man and wife,
He burst forth, goaded, "Some day I will leave—
Leave you forever!" And his father stared,
Lifted and clenched his hand, but let it unloose,
Nerveless. The blow, unstruck, yet quivered through
The boy's whole body.

        Waiting for the night,
Reuben made ready, lifted latch, went forth;
Then, with his little bundle in his hand,
Took the bleak road that led him to the world.
When Jerry eighteen years had sailed, had bared
His hurt soul to the pitiless sun and drunk
The rainy brew of storms on all seas, tired
Of wreck and fever and renewed mischance
That would not end in death, a longing stirred
Within him to revisit that gray coast
Where he was born. He landed at the port
Whence first he sailed; and, as in fervid youth,
Set forth upon the highway, to walk home.
Some hoarding he had made, wherewith to enrich
His brother's brood for spendthrift purposes;
And as he walked he wondered how they looked,
How tall they were, how many there might be.
At noon he set himself beside the way,
Under a clump of willows sprouting dense
O'er the weed-woven margin of a brook;
While in the fine green branches overhead
Song-sparrows lightly perched, for whom he threw
From his scant bread some crumbs, remembering well
Old days when he had played with birds like these—

The same, perhaps, or grandfathers of theirs,
Or earlier still progenitors: whereat
They chirped and chattered louder than before.
But, as he sat, a boy came down the road,
Stirring the noontide dust with laggard feet.
Young Reuben 't was, who seaward made his way.
And Jerry hailed him, carelessly, his mood
Moving to salutation, and the boy,
From under his torn hat-brim looking, answered.
Then, seeing that he eyed his scrap of bread,
The sailor bade him come and share it. So
They fell to talk; and Jerry, with a rough,
Quick-touching kindness, the boy's heart so moved
That unto him he all his wrong confessed.
Gravely the sailor looked at him, and told
His own tale of mad flight and wandering; how,
Wasted he had come back, his life a husk
Of withered seeds, a raveled purse, though once
With golden years well stocked, all squandered now.
At ending, he prevailed, and Reub was won
To turn and follow. Jerry, though he knew
Not yet the father's name, said he that way
Was going, too, and he would intercede
Between the truant and his father. Back
Together then they went. But on the way,
As now they passed from pines to farming-land,
The boy asked more. "'T is queer you should have come
From these same parts, and run away like me!
You did not tell me how it happened."

JERRY.

                    Foolish,
All of it! But I thought it weightier
Than the world's history, once. I could not stay
And see my brother married to the girl

I loved; and so I went.

THE BOY.

                    I had an uncle
That was in love. But he — he drowned himself.
Why do men do so?

JERRY.

   Drowned himself? And when?

THE BOY.

I don't know. Long ago; it's like a dream
To me. I was not born then. Deacon Snow
Has told me something of it. Mother cries
Even now, beside his grave. Poor uncle!

JERRY.

   His grave! (*That* could not be, then.) Yet if it should be, How can I
think Grace cried —

THE BOY.

                 How did you know
My mother's name was Grace?

JERRY.

>   I am confused
> By what you say. But is your mother's name
> Grace? How! Grace, too?

>   A strange uneasiness
> In Jerry's breast had waked. They walked awhile
> In silence. This he could not well believe,
> That Grace and Reuben unhappy were, nor that
> One son alone was theirs. Therefore aside
> He thrust that hidden, sharp foreboding: still
> He trusted, still sustained a calm suspense,
> And ranged among his memories. "Tell me, son,"
> He said, "about this Deacon Snow — Rob Snow
> It must be, I suppose."

THE BOY.

>   Oh, do you know him?

JERRY.

> A deacon now! Ay, once I knew Rob Snow —
> A jolly blade, if ever any was,
> And merry as the full moon.

THE BOY.

>   He has failed
> A good deal now, though, since his wife died.

JERRY.

What!
(Of course; of course; all's changed.) He married!

THE BOY.

Why,
How long you must have been away! For since
I can remember he has had a wife
And children. She was Gran'ther Hungerford's—

JERRY.

Her name was Ruth?

THE BOY.

Yes, Ruth! 'T is after her
The deacon's nicest daughter's named; *she's* Ruth.

Then sadly Jerry pondered, and no more
Found speech. They tramped on sternly. To the brow
Of a long hill they came, whence they could see
The village and blue ocean; then they sank
Into a region of low-lying fields
Half-naked from the scythe, and others veined
With vines that 'midst dismantled, fallen corn
Dragged all athwart a weight of tawny gourds,
Sun-mellowed, sound. And now the level way
Stretched forward eagerly, for hard ahead
It made the turn that rounded Reuben's house.
Between the still road and the tossing sea
Lay the wide swamp, with all its hundred pools
Reflecting leaden light; anon they passed

A farm-yard where the noisy chanticleer
Strutted and ruled, as one long since had done;
And then the wayside trough with jutting spout
Of ancient, mossy wood, that still poured forth
Its liquid largess to all comers. Soon
A slow cart met them, filled with gathered kelp:
The salt scent seemed a breath of younger days.
They reached the road-bend, and the evening shone
Upon them, calmly. Jerry paused, o'erwhelmed.
Reuben, surprised, glanced at him, and then said,
"Yonder's the house." Old Jerry gazed on him,
And trembled; for before him slowly grew
Through the boy's face the mingled features there
Of father and of mother—Grace's mouth,
Ripe, pouting lips, and Reuben's square-framed eyes.
But, mastering well his voice, he bade the boy
Wait by the wall, till he a little while
Went forward, and prepared. So Reuben stayed;
And Jerry with uncertain step advanced,
As dreaming of his youth and this his home.
Slowly he passed between the gateless posts
Before the unused front door, slowly too
Beyond the side porch with its woodbine thick
Draping autumnal splendor. Thus he came
Before the kitchen window, where he saw
A gray-haired woman bent o'er needle-work
In gathering twilight. And without a voice,
Rooted, he stood. He stirred not, but his glance
Burned through the pane; uneasily she turned,
And seeing that shaggy stranger standing there
Expectant, shook her head, as though to warn
Some chance, wayfaring beggar. He, though, stood
And looked at her immovably. Then, quick
The sash upthrowing, she made as if to speak
Harshly; but still he held his quiet eyes
Upon her. Now she paused; her throat throbbed full;
Her lips paled suddenly, her wan face flamed,
A fertile stir of memory strove to work
Renewal in those features wintry cold.

And so she hung, while Jerry by a step
Drawn nearer, coming just beneath her, said,
"Grace!" And she murmured, "Jerry!" Then she bent
Over him, clasping his great matted head
With those worn arms, all joyless; and the tears
Fell hot upon his forehead from her eyes.
For now in this dim gloaming their two souls
Unfruited, by an instant insight wild,
Delicious, found the full, mysterious clew
Of individual being, each in each.
But, tremulously, soon they drew themselves
Away from that so sweet, so sad embrace,
The first, the last that could be theirs. Then he,
Summing his story in a word, a glance,
Added, "But though you see me broken down
And poor enough, not empty-handed quite
I come. For God set in my way a gift,
The best I could have sought. I bring it you
In memory of the love I bore. Not now
Must that again be thought of! Waste and black
My life's fields lie behind me, and a frost
Has stilled the music of my hopes, but here
If I may dwell, nor trouble you, such a joy
Were mine, I dare not ask it. Oh forgive
The weakness! Come and see my gift!"

               Ah, tears
Flowed fast, that night, from springs of love unsealed
Once more within the ancient house — rare tears
Of reconciliation, grief, and joy!
A miracle, it seemed, had here been wrought,
The dead brought back to life. And with him came
The prodigal, repenting.

               So, thenceforth,
A spirit of peace within the household dwelt.
In Jerry a swift-sent age these years had brought,
To soften him, wrought with all the woe at home

Such open, gracious dignity, that all
For cheer and guidance learned to look to him.
But chiefly th' younger Reuben sought his aid,
And he with homely wisdom shaped the lad
To a life's loving duty. Yet not long,
Alas! the kind sea-farer with them stayed.
After some years his storm-racked body drooped.
The season came when crickets cease to sing
And flame-curled leaves fly fast; and Jerry sank
Softly toward death. Then, on a boisterous morn
That beat the wrecked woods with incessant gusts
To wrest some last leaf from them, he arose
And passed away. But those who loved him watched
His fading, half in doubt, and half afraid,
As if he must return again; for now
Entering the past he seemed, and not a life
Beyond; and some who thought of that old grave
In the orchard, dreamed a breath's space that the man
Long buried had come back, and could not die.
But so he died, and, ceasing, made request
Beside that outcast of the deep to lie.
None other mark desired he but the stone
Set there long since, though at a stranger's grave,
In heavy memory of him thought dead.

They marked the earth with one more mound beside
The other, near a gap in the low wall
That looked out seaward. There you ever hear
The deep, remorseful requiem of the sea;
And there, in autumn, windfalls, showering thick
Upon the grave, score the slow, voiceless hours
With unrebounding stroke. All round about
Green milkweed rankly thrives, and golden-rod
Sprouts from his prostrate heart in fine-poised grace
Of haughty curve, with every crest in flower.